Book 1

Hello!

by Francie Alexander
Illustrated by Vincent Andriani

SCHOLASTIC

I see .
Cat

Hello! Hello!

2

I see .

Dog

Hello!

Hello!

3

I see .
Rabbit

Hello!   Hello!

4

I see .

Bear

Hello!

Hello!

I see .

Hippo

Hello!   Hello!

6

I see.

Hello!

My Words

*hello

*I

*see

*new high frequency words